Scattered Sayings

I smiled but you looked away,
and you chose to play me instead.
I wanted to leave but I chose to stay,
now I feel like drowning every day.
I need someone to numb my pain.
You never cared, it was all just games,
but maybe losing you was what I gained.

I'm starting to believe that what I'm feeling is permanent,
and it makes me feel stupid that I cared so much when you didn't.
After every single lie that I let pass by,
After all the times that you've made me cry,
I threw it all behind and still managed to smile when I looked you in the eye.
Now you've got me reminiscing, I've overdosed on your love,
and every time you pulled me in, I got the chills from your touch.
I was blinded,
I should've had caution tapes around my heart.

Why does every love song remind me of you?
Why does my heart lead me back to you?
Tell me why I love you even though I've felt used?
You made me feel special,
Then you made me feel blue,
But all you truly ever did was break my heart in two.

You ask me why I always expect heartbreak,
You ask me why I always the worst,
You ask me why I'm always having doubts,
But it's not my fault that letdowns, broken promises, and heartbreak is what I've always experienced.
You promised, "I won't leave and I intend on leaving that promise".
But where are you now? Because my smile is as fake as your promise.

Sometimes I want people to hurt me,
so I can feel less for them,
so I can be able to move on.
But no matter how much he hurt me,
it never made me feel less for him and I'm not moved on.
I guess that's what we call love.

It's nights like these where I miss you terribly and start wondering if you even miss me,
if you even miss me just a little?
Do you miss the way that I used to comfort you?
The way I'd hold you through the nights.
The times I cared for you.
The times I cried for you.
The times I missed sleep to make sure that you're okay.
But look at you now,
partying,
kissing,
and dancing with strangers.
You don't need me anymore.
Do you?

Sometimes you're just better off not knowing.
You're better off not knowing what they did or how they're feeling.
You're better off not knowing whether they're doing well without you,
or if they're a bit sadder, now that you're gone.
You're better off not knowing if they were partying on a Friday night,
or if they woke up next to someone new on a Saturday morning.
Not knowing if they still have sleepless nights or not.
You're better off not knowing if they're with someone else or not.
You're better off not knowing.
You're better off worrying about yourself and finding yourself instead of finding unnecessary answers to unnecessary questions that do you no good.

Your name doesn't mean anything to me anymore.
I didn't forget you, I don't think I ever will.
But now I think about you a little less.
You don't make me sad anymore.
My heart doesn't skip a beat and I don't get butterflies when I see you.
You're not the first thing I think about when I wake up in the morning anymore.
That perfume I wear doesn't remind me of you anymore.
The places we used to go to make me less sad, not completely.
And when I listen to sad songs, I don't cry as much as I used to.
And you know what?
It feels good to be freed from something that was both your poison and your medicine at the same time.
You're not my poison or my medicine anymore.
You're just another story to be told.
A person I had memories with.
I don't regret you, I just know better.
You know I know the real you.
So if you still can't sleep, don't hesitate to call me at 3 A.M like you used to.

Trapped in fantasies that'll never happen,
holding onto unrealistic hopes that are overlapping,
waiting for the day you'd call me in the middle of the night,
and waiting for the day my brain and my heart stop striving for a fight.
Maybe one day I'll be able to sleep.
Not awake to the thought of you,
and not having you in my dreams.
I hope you find love,
a love so deep.
Makes you forget all your hurt,
and loves you even at your worst.
Goodnight babe, I'll miss the warmth of your heartbeat.

I pass by you in the halls,
Knowing your secrets and all your flaws.
But now you're just a stranger with memories,
guess that means we weren't meant to be.
I pass by you and almost want to smile,
but then I remember, we haven't talked in a while.
Does your heart ache as mine does?
Were you heartbroken like I was?
Do you not warm up to anyone like I do, just because simply they aren't you?

I guess that being too careful doesn't do much good in the end,
because these days I wake up and it's hard to get out of bed,
and when I try to close my eyes I end up reminiscing over what we could have been.
Was my love even enough to begin with?
You were "lost" and "confused".
I was loyal and committed.
After all, *"you don't know what you have till it's gone"* is true.
You're back now.
It just hit you, you lost me.

Sometimes I wonder, was it real? Or was it all an act?
Did you really feel things or was it just a game?
Did I waste my time and energy or was it all real and worth it?
I'm hoping it was because now I can't seem to love again.
My heart is broken and I don't know if it'll get fixed.
I guess I'll never know, but I do know that every word I said,
I said it out of the truth.
And that's the only thing that I don't regret.

I was art long before you started to admire me.
I was full long before I made a space for you in my heart.
I was bright long before you lit me up.
I don't need you to make me feel enough.

You showed me all of your flaws and your scars,
I took you as you are.
I embraced your imperfections.
But don't you ever dare,
to try and knock me down,
or point out my imperfections just to make yourself feel better.
Never.
Because who are you to point out my flaws when I accepted yours?
Who are you to make me feel less when I put you on top?
I don't need you to make me feel enough,
and you won't make me feel less than enough,
even if you try.

Hearts and Colours

Your words cut right through my skin,
they managed to rip my heart out.
I used to believe your "I love you's" every second,
without a doubt.
I used to associate you with the colour white,
so pure and so clear.
But now your words make me wonder if you have a different colour,
an unpleasant one.
The one that cost me tears.
I can't associate you with a colour anymore because you got me wishing I was colourblind.
I've been looking for the spark in your eyes,
lately, that's been hard to find.

How does it feel, breaking my heart again?
Does it help your weak ego, or decrease your self-consciousness and insecurities?
Do you really love me like you claim to do, or am I just another game of yours?
You love winning, don't you?
Why are you still claiming to love me and be with me if you got what you wanted?
Is your ego still hungry?
Do you have more things left to prove?
Didn't you already get what you wanted?
You must love the fact that even after breaking me once, you're breaking me again.
I don't blame you.
I blame myself for letting you in.

Sometimes out of nowhere,
when I'm having a clear mind and a good day,
the trust issues start showing up again.
I suppress them as they crawl through my skin and into my head.
Yet, I remind myself, *they're just in my head.*
He's in my head.
It's all in my head.
It's okay, calm down.
Not every man will hurt.
Not every man will lie.
But some feelings just die.
And that's okay,
because you can't possibly be a love-giving machine when all you've ever received was hurt.
Even if he loves you properly now,
what's a fire extinguisher going to do when the house has already been burnt?

Forcefully Hoping

I can't force you to love me,
I can't force you to care.
But I hope,
that love is a strong enough force,
that makes you want to stay.

Your Mind

Tell me what goes on in your mind,
when you tell me pretty little lies?
Do you not see the love in my eyes?
Do you forget about the times that I've cried?
It's like you're a demon in disguise,
yet you still have the nerve to act like you're surprised.
So tell me, what goes on in your mind
when you tell me pretty little lies.

Roses and Thorns

You made roses grow in my body,
forgetting that they also have thorns.
I'm waiting for those roses to die,
because I can't be this hurt anymore.

The Paradoxes in Loving Him

You hate how nervous he makes you feel,
yet you love it because it tells you that what you feel for him is real.
You hate it when he stares at you because it makes you shy,
yet you love it because you can see the sparks in his eyes.
You love the way he kisses you,
like you're air and he can't breathe,
but you're scared that he's going to be the only air you'll ever need.

Inspiration and Tears

I say sadness is my inspiration for writing.
I've turned you into poems every time I was sad,
romanticized the pain,
made you my beautiful yet messy agony.
I wonder what type of poetry I could turn you into if happiness was my inspiration.
Because every tear I shed is worth a word.
I wonder what I could write, and how many words I could write with all the smiles you've
brought me.

Art is my escape.
But I can't escape you, because you're my art.

Love vs. Addiction

Maybe I don't love you.
Maybe I'm just addicted to you.
Because love is supposed to add to your happiness,
it's supposed to make you feel better about yourself.
It's supposed to calm your anxiousness,
but I'm not feeling any of that.
Maybe I'm just worried that I won't find someone that makes me feel the way you do.
People don't love drugs,
they're just addicted to them because they love the way they make them feel.
I guess you're my drug.

Trust issues

Inside my rib-cage town,
there's a house haunted by the ghosts of those who I trusted.
But I can't handle the paranoia anymore,
go find another home.
These trust issues are eating me alive,
I am hoping they find
something other than my body to prey on.

I saw the way you talked about her.
My heart dropped.
Now I see you as a monster.
I couldn't help but think,
that maybe one day,
you'd talk about me the same way.

Senses

Can you hear the silence?
Even when it's loud?
Can you taste the pain?
Whether it's the saltiness that falls down your cheek,
or the sound of the sky when it rains?
Can you see the scars?
Even when they're faded?
Can you smell the catastrophe that's been created?
Can you touch the sky?
Even if it's far up high?
Or is that only possible,
the moment that you die?

I remember when you said to me,
that if God can forgive, then who are we not to forgive?
I told you that I forgive but I don't forget.
Yet you seem to forget that I am not as merciful as God.
And I am not like Jesus,
I won't die for your sins.
You seem to forget that the scars might be light on my skin,
but trust me, they are much deeper within.
I will forgive but I will not forget the way that I was shattered.
I will forgive but I will not forget how you showed that I was the last thing that mattered,
just so you could feel temporarily flattered.
So forgive me for not moving on from the past.
Forgive me for giving up on the hope that one day, maybe we would last.
Darling, I told you, I am made of glass.
I break and I shatter,
and now it's turned into a battle.
A battle between me and myself.
I warned you once,
and I warned you twice.
And after all the chances that I've given,
you still seem to believe that my heart's made of ice?
But again, I apologize.
I apologize for not having it in me to commit to a heart that I tried fixing,
when all it ever did was break me.
I apologize for accepting your love but denying your efforts of allowing me to trust.
But please, believe me when I say that it's not you, it's me.
I wanted to stay, but it looks like I need to leave.

How could you possibly be so blind,
to the way, I see you in my eyes?
I'm the one who notices the slightest bit of change in your tone.
I'm the one who'd share your pain if you'd let me.
I'm the one who notices the waves of sadness that fill up your eyes.
I'm the one who knows that you're lying when you say "I'm fine".
Loving you at your worst,
and trying to heal all your hurt.
Wanting to pull the sadness out of you,
and fill you with love,
the way you fill an empty cup.
I'm sorry if my love isn't enough,
but at least I'm trying.
I've been trying.

Can't you see?
It's you.
It has always been you.
I promised myself to never let you back in,
but now you're buried so deep in my heart you've left a scar that's hard to fade.
No matter how many times I've told myself I'd let you go,
a part of me hoped you'd stay,
and so you did.
No matter how many times I told myself that I'm better off without you,
I find myself writing about you.
I've tried being with someone else but you were always in the back of my mind.
You gave me a different type of butterflies.
So why are you so blind,
to the way that I see you in my eyes?

Love?

Love?
You don't lie to the people you love.
You don't leave them wondering whether they should believe you or believe what their body is telling them to believe.
You don't manipulate the people you love, you don't treat them as if they're worthless.
You don't make them choose between you or themselves.
An apology is appreciated, yes, but it doesn't mean that it doesn't still hurt.
Every time you look back, it still hurts you, doesn't it?
You said you forgive them, right?
Because that's what you do for the people you love, you forgive them.
You give them second chances, even when they've ripped your heart out of your chest.
You don't want to lose them but it doesn't mean that it doesn't hurt.
I know I said I forgive you, but it doesn't mean that my heart doesn't break into billions of pieces every time I think about what you've done.
I'm sorry if I'm reminding you of the past, but
I can't help but wonder if you love me,
or if you love the idea of me,
or the feeling that I give you.
I gave you all of me,
but sometimes, we give the right parts of us to the wrong people because
it all comes down to "love", right?

Love vs. Addiction 2.0

He doesn't send you a good morning text, knowing that the little things matter to you,
but you love him, so it's okay, right?
He ghosts you for days, knowing that you're attached to him and that you overthink,
but you love him, so it's okay, right?
He doesn't give you reassurance, knowing that you have huge trust issues,
but you love him, so it's okay, right?
He decides to hit you up after midnight when he's done with his day, knowing that you want to be prioritized,
but you love him, so it's okay, right?

Because for love, you're willing to do anything, right?
But darling, what you don't realize is that this isn't love.
Love doesn't hurt.
Love is not pain.
Love doesn't leave you wondering if you're good enough.
Love doesn't drain your energy and give you more tears to cry than smiles to wear.
Maybe he's just your addiction and you're just too scared to admit it.
Maybe you don't love him.
Maybe you're addicted to him.
Maybe you're addicted to the feeling of butterflies running in your stomach every time you see him or the way he caresses your body.
But love is supposed to add to your happiness,
it's supposed to make you feel better about yourself.
It's supposed to calm your anxiousness, but you're not feeling any of that.
Maybe you're just worried that you won't find someone who makes you feel the way that he does.
I mean, come on, people don't love drugs.
They're just addicted to them because they love the way they make them feel.
And darling, don't you know?
Drugs are bad for you.
They make you feel things that aren't real,
and when you're not high anymore,
you realize that,
after all, he's just a drug and you're just addicted to him.

Losing Interest

I've been looking for more reasons to leave than reasons to stay,
'cuz I feel like you only love me every other day.
I've been trying to put my thoughts into words,
but letting you know will only make things worse.
I'm stuck between *end it before it ends you* or *just give it another chance*,
because you said you've changed,
but to be honest, I don't think it's going to last.
I feel like I don't even know if I love you anymore.
A part of me feels guilty, but I know that I've felt this before.
But is it even love to begin with when you don't know if you love the person anymore?
I've been losing interest 'cuz of the lack of consistency,
because lately we've been communicating so distantly.
Should I let go or should I give it a chance?
I mean, do you even feel a thing when you hold my hand?

The thought of you with someone else,
burns my heart and eats up my soul.
I'm so used to you being mine and only mine,
that I can't bear to think of how you're with her now.
How she's kissing the same lips that I used to kiss.
Holding the same hand I used to hold.
Burying her head on the same spot in your chest the way that I did.
Loving the heart that I used to love.

Let it hurt,
Let it bleed,
Let it burn,
Until it turns,
Into ashes.

I give,
I give,
and I give,
but I never get.
I'm running out of love.

I don't want to be taught lessons.
I want to be taught that it's okay to not be okay.
I want to be taught that sometimes,
 sweet and kind people may hurt other people,
they aren't always kind,
and that it's okay to not be okay.
I want to be taught that the people who care for you,
will be there for you.
They will always know the reasons behind your tears,
and your cries.
They will let you know that it's okay to not be okay.

Don't tell me that you miss me,
when you don't even make an effort to see me.
Don't tell me that I'm your go-to,
when you never open up to me or come to me.
Don't tell me that you love me,
when you treat me like I mean nothing to you.
Don't ask me to be happier,
when I know that all of your sweet words are lies.
Because it hurts.
I give my all,
but I get nothing at all.
It hurts to be half-loved.
So just let me go.
Let me let you go.
It hurts being half-loved.

You could cry in their chest,
You could try your best,
You could give them everything you have to lose,
And they would still turn right back around,
And do the one thing they said they wouldn't do.

Boys Like You

Boys like you don't scare me.
Boys like you can't hurt me.
Boys like you are cowards,
pathological liars.
So insecure that they feel the need to fill in that empty space in their heart with temporary
people.
Boys like you are just boys. Not men.
Boys like you can't own up to their morals,
or their words, yet still, force them on others.
Boys like you are toxic,
manipulative,
and their actions are poisonous.
Boys like you can't be alone,
they constantly feel the need to have multiple people feeding their ego.
Boys like you have a talent for rationalizing to distort the realities of their wrongdoings.
Boys like you don't know love, only lust.
Boys like you make me want to throw up in disgust.

I can't help but feel depressed.
Every morning I feel the neglect,
from sunrise to sunset.

I can't help but feel your touch.
Seems like I could never get enough.
Life without you,
life is tough.

I can't help but miss your love.
The love that I never got a hold of.
I wish you were somebody that I could trust.

Stuck

Stuck in between wanting to move on and wanting to go back.
Stuck in between wanting to find someone new,
while I sleep and wake up to the thought of you.
Why did you do this?
You drained the trust out of my blood,
and left me here with lust.
You left me lusting for your love.

Actually, you didn't leave me.
You made me leave you.
You made me walk away.
It took every single bit of courage in me.
Every thought in my brain.
Every nerve in my system.
Every gut in my body.
Every pit in my stomach.
Every tear in my eye.
And every muscle in my tongue,
to finally say *no* to you.
To finally put me first.
Is this what a person like me deserves?
To have their heart broken by the same person?
Not once, but twice.
I wish I could heal the bruises you left with ice.
But it's not like I can go back to saying *I love you* without feeling the words choke me up.
Because if you really loved me back, why would you have me begging for your love?
Asking for your time,
asking for your attention,
when I had the purest types of intentions.
Then you make me feel bad for leaving when it's the only form of healing.
I mean, how much hurt can a heart really take?
If loving you was a mistake,
then it would be the best and worst one I've ever made.

Hurt Me

Hurt me more so I could write a little more.
Hurt me more so I could take this pain and turn it into art.
Hurt me more so I don't have to feel bad about walking away.
Hurt me more so I could write a little less.
Keep on hurting me until I become heartless.

One of the worst feelings a human being could experience,
is going through the process of healing,
and thinking that they've moved on and healed,
just to break down all over again.
Over one word.
A promise that wasn't kept,
and a single memory.

You took the kindness of my heart for granted after all,
and I won't take you back,
even if you make the skies fall.

My heart took enough damage.
My heart took enough hurt.
Tell me, why do I still miss you?
Is it the way that my body works?

Love to me has been re-defined in every single way.
I don't know what to do anymore.
But I can't take any more of your mistakes.

You're the first thing that I've ever gotten stuck on,
and I'll always be there for you,
because I don't think I'll ever want you gone.

Toxic

Now I'm the toxic one.
After all the chances I've given,
I'm the toxic one.
After all the gaslighting and manipulation,
after the constant lying and my dedication,
I'm the toxic one.
I'm the one that can't move on.
I've been lied to and stripped of my confidence,
I've been losing my consciousness.
I've been trying to figure out how I'm feeling
and I'm stuck in between staying or leaving.
Leaving my heart-breaker,
or staying with the only one that was able to break through my heart.

When you feel like crying,
and there's no one there to numb the pain,
hold back your tears.
Don't let them fall.
Just take a pill, and watch the rain.
Fall back and relax,
as you watch the sky cry on your behalf.
Suppress your feelings and forget about healing.
Ignore your problems and pretend like you're happy.
No one likes a sad girl,
so just numb your pain and hope for the day where feeling is not going to be an issue anymore.

Is that the thunder?
Or is that the sound of my heart trembling as I blast my ears with songs that remind me of the
years where our love wasn't gone?
The years where you didn't go looking for ways to fix yourself by breaking me.
It seems like it was a dream far from reality and everything that happened,
happened so magically,
There are magical feelings and then there's black magic,
I forgot about the black magic part, maybe that's why the ending was so tragic.

As two hearts once collided,
one chose to overpower and break the other.
Although it may surprise you,
the heart that was broken had always been stronger than the one who broke it. You may ask why?
Well, that's because that heart didn't mind being broken.
It let itself feel.

You ask me why I'm always doubting your love,
but darling, how am I supposed to believe that you love me when you can't even be true to me?
or true to yourself?
You ask me for how long am I going to be doubting your love for me,
Here's my answer to you,
As long as you're loving the person that you want me to be.
The image in your head.
Not the person that I am.

Away

Your version of the full truth turned out to be half of your lie.
You looked me in the eyes and lied a million times.
And oh, what an amazing feeling now that you're finally out of my mind.
turns out you weren't only oblivious when it came to my feelings
but how foolish of you to think that the full truth wouldn't be revealing?
Revealing by night and day.
I don't regret the moments that I chose to stay,
because after all the times you've played your games,
I'm finally so relieved that you're away.

p.s - I always find out x

The parties are over now, and you have no one to love.
You lust over her, but you know that I'm the only one you could trust.
I read you like a book,
I read between the lines.
I know when you lie, every time you say "I'm fine".
Yet that doesn't satisfy you enough?
I know that for a fact and that's because,
your lips were able to reach another's while you were still in love with me.
You were kissing her softly while I was in the back of your mind.
You were kissing her in the back of your car while I was hurting inside.
But you kiss me like I'm air and you can't breathe.
I guess that this is what puts my heart at ease.

Insecure men cheat.
And when they get caught, that's when they want to speak.
Some of us fall for their lies,
and it just repeats.
Until one day you decide,
that's when I'm going to leave.
Because you've been crying yourself to sleep.
You've been starving but can't even eat.
All you can think of is the heat,
the heat of his body pulling against yours.
Hands held.
Chest to chest.
His tongue on your neck.
Thinking that it was okay because you love him,
but that's when it hits you: *he's been with her too.*
You look at yourself in the mirror and try to swallow your sorrow.
You look at yourself in disgust,
because now you have a body that's been touched,
touched by his dirty hands.
His lying lips.
His distasteful tongue.
His shameful eyes,
and again you realize, *he's a demon in disguise.*
He always has and always been,
a boy that's empty from within.

You've wiped his tears,
you know his fears.
You've eased his pain,
and that shall remain,
the memory carved into his brain,
that he will try so hard to get out.
Because he couldn't handle a woman that was filled with love,
when he was filled with hate.

It's the way that life is, you know?
She breaks your heart, then you break mine.
I fall apart, but then I give it some time.
I'm hurting inside, but I tell you I'm fine.
I try to fix you while you're breaking me.
Do I keep you in, or do I set you free?
I come and I go, but I never leave.
I'm dealing with a heart that I didn't break,
and forgiving you for all of your mistakes.
I'm putting up with all of the headaches,
and the nights that my heart aches.

People call it toxic,
but I call it karmic.
Some say it's chaotic,
I say it's symbolic.
You lie to me and blame it on your trauma,
I confront you then you tell me you're done with all this drama,
I cry and I yell, you say I'm being unreal.
You make me feel like it's a sin to feel.
You make me feel like I'm crazy,
yet you break my trust on a daily.
Your past is traumatic,
yet you keep wandering,
you're like a nomadic.
Trying to find that one piece that fits,
but every time, you seem to miss.
You keep on coming back,
thinking it would last.
And I keep on letting you in.
Do you really love me?
Or are you just filling the void that's within?

I've tried laughing in the places that I've cried at,
I've tried changing the narrative.
I've tried making new memories in the places that have our names written all over them.
However, it seems like the ink was dug in a little too deep.
It seems like everytime I try to rewrite our story,
it all ends the same,
it all ends in pain.

You said you could find a hundred reasons to why you love me,
yet you couldn't find one reason to not lie to me.

You're asking me to let go as if it's as easy as the wind flows.
All that hurt,
the sorrow,
the anger,
and the sadness that built up inside of me that caused my heart to feel like it's getting stung by millions of bees,
how do you expect me to just "let go"?
It's hard for you to understand because you were never in my shoes,
and maybe I'm being profound but letting go is harder than getting out of bed,
or trying to fall asleep without a pill.
Don't you think that I would've let go a long time if I could've?

Special

You used to call me beautiful,
and I'd believe you.
Because you made me feel like the only girl in this world.
You still call me beautiful,
but I've seen how these 9 letters roll off your tongue so easily,
when you say it to her,
while you were still in love with me.
Now I don't feel anything when you call me beautiful.
I just feel like one of the many girls in this world

I loved you with everything that I had.
You broke me with everything that you had.
I loved you in every way I could.
You broke me in every way you could.
You say you love me,
but love is not supposed to hurt.

I killed a part of me to keep you close,
but it took the death of hope for me to let you go.

The End?

I hope you're doing well.
I hope you're okay.
I hope your heart is at peace knowing that I forgive you for not knowing better at the time.
I hope you know I understand.
Don't hurt yourself, please.
After all, I thank you for allowing me to view this world from a different perspective.
They say that some things break your heart but fix your vision.
And I'd rather have a good vision than have a heart.
I hope you know that it took everything in me to do this.
The timing was off, if I could sum it up to you I'd say it was too late.
Everything was too late,
and I was drained.
Drained and stripped of everything I had to offer.
I do appreciate every little thing though.
I'm doing well.
Better actually.
You deserve what you have to offer.
You truly deserve good things.
I'm sorry that good thing couldn't be me.
I tried.
I forgive you.
Not that I would expect the need to be forgiven,
but I hope you forgive me too.
-x.o

Made in the USA
Monee, IL
22 May 2021